The Berenstain Bears'

FUNNY VALENTINE

It may be chilly outside
when Valentine's Day comes,
but little bears warm up
and send cards to their chums.

The Berenstain Bears'

FUNNY VALENTINE

Stan & Jan Berenstain

Random House 🏠 New York

Copyright © 2002 by Berenstain Enterprises, Inc.

All rights reserved. Published in the United States by Random House Children's Books,
a division of Penguin Random House LLC, New York. Originally published in
slightly different form by Random House Children's Books, New York, in 2002.

Random House and the colophon are registered trademarks of
Penguin Random House LLC.

Visit us on the Web! • rhcbooks.com • BerenstainBears.com

Library of Congress Cataloging-in-Publication Data
Berenstain, Stan. The Berenstain Bears' funny valentine / Stan & Jan Berenstain.
p. cm.
Summary: As Valentine's Day approaches, Sister hopes for
more attention from one boy and less from another.
ISBN 978-0-375-81126-5 (trade)
[1. Valentine's Day—Fiction. 2. Bears—Fiction.]
I. Berenstain, Jan. II. Title. III. Series: Berenstain, Stan. First time books.
PZ7.B4483 Beng 2003 [E]—dc21 2002013400

Printed in the United States of America

31 30 29 28 27 26 25 24 23 22

Random House Children's Books supports the First Amendment
and celebrates the right to read.

Sister Bear and her friends were jumping rope during recess. They were jumping partly to keep warm because it was February and partly because they loved to jump rope. Sister and Lizzy were turning and Amy was jumping.

"Uh-oh!" said Lizzy. "There's a boy coming over from the boys' side of the playground, and guess who it is."

There wasn't any rule about a boys' side and a girls' side at Bear Country School. But the boys did sort of stay on one side of the playground and the girls on the other.

Oh! I hope it's Herbie Cubbison! thought Sister. Sister Bear liked Herbie, and everybody knew it—except maybe Herbie.

"Is it Herbie?" asked Sister, not wanting to look.

"No," said Lizzy. "It's Billy Grizzwold."

"Oh, no! Not that awful Billy Grizzwold!" said Sister, turning the rope faster and faster.

"Hey, slow down," said Amy.
"Hi, Sister!" said Billy.

"Don't you 'hi' me," said Sister, "and you better not have a worm, like you did yesterday, or a dead mouse, like you did the day before!"

"No worm. No dead mouse," said Billy. "Just me!" And with that he began jumping with Amy and got tangled in the rope.

Down they all fell in a heap.
"Why, you . . . !" said Sister. She
pulled the rope free and ran after Billy.
Sister was a fast runner. But Billy was
faster and kept just ahead of her.

Oh, why doesn't Herbie Cubbison come to my rescue? thought Sister as she chased Billy around and around the playground.

Herbie was too busy playing fistball even to notice.

Then the bell rang and
they all went back to class.

"Well, class," said Teacher Jane. "As I guess you all know, Valentine's Day is coming. We're going to have a valentine party with punch and cookies, and we're all going to give valentines to each other."

"Yippee!" cried the class.

"Oh, yeah?" said Sister under her breath. "If she thinks I'm going to send a valentine to that no-good, rotten Billy Grizzwold, she's got another think coming." But Sister had another think coming, too. She began to think about what kind of valentine Herbie Cubbison might send her.

She was still thinking about it that night at dinner when the phone rang.

"It's probably for you, Brother," said Papa. "So you might as well answer it."

"That's right," said Sister. "It's probably one of your sweethearts."

"You cut that out!" said Brother as he went to answer the phone.

"I wish you wouldn't tease your brother like that," said Mama.

"Well," said Sister when Brother returned, "which one of your sweethearts was it, Bonnie, Jill, or Alexis?"

"It was Bonnie, if you must know," said Brother, "and she was calling about math homework."

"Uh-huh," said Sister. "But that's not the real reason she was calling. The real reason is that Valentine's Day is coming and she wants to make sure you send her an icky-sticky valentine with lots of kisses."

"You cut that out!" shouted Brother. "Mama, if she doesn't cut that out, I'm gonna—"

But the phone rang again.
"It's probably Jill this time,"
said Sister as Brother went to
the phone.

"My dear," said Mama, "there's nothing wrong with Brother having friends who happen to be girls. And there's nothing wrong with Valentine's Day."

"Your mama's right," said Papa. "And not only that, I seem to recall that Teacher Jane has a valentine party every year, and I bet you're going to get a whole *bunch* of valentines yourself."

"That's right," said Sister. "But that's because we have to. Teacher Jane's got a rule."

It was true. There were twenty-four cubs in Sister's class, and every cub had to send a valentine to every other cub. They didn't have to be expensive and you could make them if you wanted to. Sister thought she might just make one for that no-good, rotten Billy Grizzwold. She began to think about what it might say.

"A penny for your thoughts," said Mama.
"Er—uh," said Sister, "I was just thinking
of a valentine to send to Billy Grizzwold."

"Is Billy a *special* friend of yours?" asked Mama.

"A special friend?" said Sister, her eyes flashing. "Does a friend knock you down when you're jumping rope? Does a friend chase after you with a dead mouse? Does a friend put a hop toad in your lunch box?"

"I suppose not," said Mama. "But—"

"There are no *buts* about it, Mama," continued Sister. "That Billy Grizzwold is a no-good nuisance and if he doesn't stop bothering me . . ."

"Why don't you ask your boyfriend, Herbie Cubbison, to make him stop?" said Brother, who had come back to the table.

"Boyfriend? *Boyfriend?*" shouted Sister. "You take that back!"

"Everyone knows that Sister Bear has a huge crush on Herbie Cubbison."

"Mama, make him take that back!" cried Sister. "I've hardly ever said a word to Herbie Cubbison! Brother's the big valentine sweetheart around here."

"That'll be quite enough!" said Papa.
"Valentine's Day is supposed to be fun.
It's not supposed to be a shouting match."

"Well, I'll stop if he'll stop," grumped
Sister.

"And I'll stop if she'll stop," grouched
Brother.

Papa put a finger to his lips
and they both stopped.

Sister didn't have to make a special valentine for Billy Grizzwold. She found the perfect one for him at the card store.

It showed a scary-looking Frankenbear-type monster with a bolt on each side of his neck. It said:

*Monsters come in
every shape and size.
But when it comes to creepy,
you take the prize!*

She'd sign it, "Guess Who." She couldn't wait to see Billy's face when he opened it at the class Valentine's Day party.

But Sister forgot to watch when Billy opened her valentine because among the valentines she received was one that took her breath away. It was all hearts and flowers and inside it said, "Will you be my special friend?"

"Wow!" said Lizzy Bruin. "It must have cost a whole dollar!"

"It's signed, 'Guess Who,'" said Sister. "Who do you suppose it's from?"

"Well, I know who you *hope* it's from," said Lizzy.

"If somebody sent *me* a beautiful valentine that cost a whole dollar, I'd sure want to know who it was from. There's Herbie over by the punch bowl. Go ask him."

Sister started for the punch bowl, but Billy Grizzwold blocked her way. He had the valentine Sister had sent him.

"I'll be glad to get you some punch," said Billy.

"And throw it down my back?" said Sister.

"No, nothing like that," said Billy. "I'm sorry about all the stuff I did. And I really don't blame you for sending me this. It's really pretty funny. How'd you like that valentine I sent you?"

"*You* sent me?" said Sister. "*You sent me this valentine?*"

"Yep," said Billy. "I saved up for weeks to get it."

Sister was confused. She didn't know what to say, so she just said, "Thanks."

She was still confused that evening when she showed Billy's valentine to Mama.

"Well, it certainly is beautiful," said Mama, "and I understand your puzzlement. It takes me back to when I was a cub your age. There was this awful boy, just like Billy Grizzwold. He was just awful. The things he did! One time he chased me with a thousand-legger."

"Yuck!" said Sister.

"And that wasn't the worst of it," continued Mama. "Once he put a giant bullfrog in my lunch box. It scared me half to death when it jumped out. It scared the whole class. It got me in a peck of trouble."

"How about that awful boy?" asked Sister. "Didn't he get in trouble?"

"Oh, yes. From time to time!" said Mama. "But after a while, he straightened out, got married, and raised a family. He became a solid citizen."

"Do I know him?" asked Sister.

"Yes," said Mama. "He's sitting right over there. It was your papa." Sister looked over at Papa, whose face was buried in the newspaper.

The next day, Billy Grizzwold came over to Sister at recess.

"Can I ask you something?" he said.

"I guess so," said Sister.

"Could we sit together at the assembly tomorrow?"

"You won't bring any worms or toads?"

"Nope," said Billy. "I promise."

"Okay," said Sister.

So the next day, Billy and Sister sat together at assembly. He brought her a flower. It was a daisy.

Sister forgot all about Herbie Cubbison.

And that afternoon, Sister pressed
Billy's daisy in a book.